TALES OF HEAVEN AND EARTH

Marc-Alain Ouaknin is a rabbi
and philosopher. He is the author
of several books about Judaism.

The British edition of this book
has been prepared with the guidance
of the Agency for Jewish Education.

Cover design by Peter Bennett

Published by Creative Education
123 South Broad Street, Mankato, Minnesota 56001
Creative Education is an imprint
of The Creative Company

Library of Congress Cataloging-in-Publication Data

Ouaknin, Marc-Alain.
[A toi je donne mes histoires. English]
I'll tell you a story / by Marc-Alain Ouaknin and Dory Rotnemer;
illustrated by Nicole Baron . . .[et al.];
translated by Sarah Matthews.
p. cm. — (Tales of heaven and earth)
Summary: The story of Maimonides, whose morality was tested by
a sultan, and other traditional Jewish tales.
ISBN 0-88682-830-9

1. Jews—Folklore. 2. Tales. [1. Jews—Folklore. 2. Folklore.]
I. Baron, Nicole, ill. II. Matthews, Sarah. III. Title.
IV. Series.
PZ8.1.0846Il   1997
398.2089924—dc20   96-32127

6 5 4 3 2 1

I'LL TELL YOU YOU A STORY

BY MARC-ALAIN OUAKNIN
AND DORY ROTNEMER
ILLUSTRATED BY NICOLE BARON,
ISABELLE FORESTIER, FRÉDÉRIC GALIMIDI,
MARIE MALLARD, ETIENNE SOUPPART

TRANSLATED BY SARAH MATTHEWS

CREATIVE EDUCATION

There was a child who could read the future better than the astrologers.

This story comes from the Midrash and was translated from the Aramaïc.

In Hebrew, letters are also numbers. The first letter, which is the number 1, is called aleph, which became *alpha* in Greek, and then A in Latin. At first, letters were little drawings, or pictograms. Aleph, which began as a drawing of an ox's head, still means ox today.

In ancient times, astrologers were asked about any important decisions. The picture below shows the constellation of Sagittarius. It is from a 14th-century manuscript on how the stars help in treating illness.

Once upon a time, in Babylon, a king wanted to build a new city. He chose a site and asked all the astrologers in his kingdom to tell him whether it was the best place. The astrologers observed the stars and told the king that it was a good site. But, they said, the city would not have good luck unless a child was offered to the king by its mother, of her own free will, to be bricked alive into the city walls.

No one came forward until, at the end of three years, an old woman did come, bringing a ten-year-

Whether a place was good or bad depended on what had happened there. A place would be holy if the people there had behaved justly and honestly.

old child. As he was about to be bricked into the wall, the child said to the king; "Oh king, let me ask your astrologers three questions. If they give the right answers, that shows that they have read the stars correctly, and I should die. If not, it shows they were wrong."

The king agreed.

"What," asked the child, "are the lightest, the sweetest, and the hardest things in the world?"

The astrologers thought hard for three days, then answered, "A feather is the lightest thing in the world, honey is the sweetest, and a stone is the hardest."

The child laughed at their reply.

"Anyone could have given an answer like that! No, the true answer is that the lightest thing in the world is a child in its mother's arms; the sweetest thing is a mother's milk on her child's lips; and the hardest thing is for a mother to offer up her child to be bricked alive into a wall."

The astrologers were ashamed, knowing they had been wrong in the advice they had given the king. The child was allowed to live.

Jewish tradition encourages people to disregard the influence of the stars and take up their freedom.

This story aims to show that people can always escape from a tragic destiny. But it also shows that people cannot base their existence on violence, and nothing can justify its use.

King Solomon had a mission to build a temple in Jerusalem . . .

This story is taken from the Midrash relating to the Book of Kings and is translated from Hebrew.

King Solomon was the third king of Israel. He ruled 3,000 years ago. The first king of Israel was Saul, the second was David, descendant of Ruth and Boaz, and the father of Solomon.

King Solomon was the wisest, richest, and most magnificent king ever to walk the earth. He had inherited many wonderful things from his father, King David, including the materials to build a temple. He longed to build it as soon as he could, but he had come up against an insoluble problem: Where was the best place to set this holiest of buildings?

The first time he had started to dig the foundations for the temple, waves as high as mountains had flooded the land and had carried off the blocks of stone. The second

The Bible tells us that David was unfit to build the temple because he was involved in war. God told David that his son Solomon would build the temple. (1 Kings, chapter 5, verse 19)

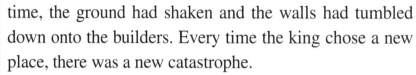

King Solomon wrote three books: Proverbs, a book of advice for life; The Song of Songs, an allegory about God and Israel; and Ecclesiastes, a book about the meaning of life.

The angel stops Abraham from sacrificing Isaac. (Painting by Rembrandt.)

time, the ground had shaken and the walls had tumbled down onto the builders. Every time the king chose a new place, there was a new catastrophe.

"How unhappy I am!" the king said sadly to himself. "How can I ever fulfill the promise I made to my father? I have already built scores of palaces, but still I have not built the House of God. How will I ever know the best place to build it?"

Solomon, in his great wisdom, could understand the language of all the animals. He asked for help from all the creatures who flew far and from those who stayed nearer home. They all replied; "Oh king, we have not found the place you are seeking."

Solomon could not sleep. One night, musing on the promise he had made, he got up from his bed and crept out of his palace. He walked through the silent streets of Jerusalem and reached the foot of Mount Moriah. He looked up and asked the stars for help, but they gave him no answer. The king, bitterly upset, leaned against an olive tree, covered his face with his hands, and wept. Suddenly, he heard a sound. Looking around him, he saw that he was in the middle of a field of freshly cut corn, and there before him was a man secretly carrying a sheaf of corn and putting

According to Jewish tradition, it was on Mount Moriah that God asked Abraham to sacrifice his son, Isaac. But God stopped Abraham from killing his son— it was a way of telling people they should not make human sacrifices, as other religions did at that time.

it in the neighboring field. He did this again and again, until fifty sheaves had been taken. The man checked that nobody had seen him and left.

"The thief," said Solomon angrily. "Come daybreak, I will find him and punish him!"

But he did not even have time to move from his place under the tree when another man arrived. The king was astonished to see this second man pick up the fifty sheaves of corn and quietly put them back in the field they had first come from!

"These two neighbors are both thieves, and I shall punish each of them severely."

Just then he heard a cricket which was sitting on a branch of the olive tree. The cricket said to Solomon, "Oh most powerful of kings, you have found the place to build your temple. Come back to this field tomorrow night and you will understand."

Solomon could hardly wait; at last his wish would be fulfilled! But first, he must find out what was happening with the two thieves.

As soon as evening fell, the king went back and sat under the tree, with the cricket for company. Toward midnight, he saw both

He found the solution, thanks to a cricket, and by watching . . .

men creeping into the field, each with a sheaf of corn. Catching sight of each other, they dropped their burdens, and stared at each other cautiously. Solomon was about to get up to stop them from attacking each other when he was amazed to see them fall into each other's arms. Unable to contain himself any longer, the king spoke to the two men, "I was here last night, and I thought to catch two thieves, but here you are embracing each other!"

The younger of the two men replied in surprise, "Lord, I have never stolen anything in my life! The corn I was carrying belongs to me, and I was putting it in my brother's field. We each inherited half of our father's field, but my brother is married and has three children to feed, while I live alone. He needs more corn than I do, so each night I take advantage of the dark to put some secretly in his field, since he will never let me give him anything."

Then the second

Olive trees are very common in Mediterranean countries. The olive branch is a symbol of peace: the dove brought news to Noah that the Flood was over by bringing him an olive branch.

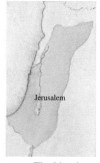

Jerusalem

The kingdom that Solomon inherited from his father, David.

God asked Solomon what he most desired, and Solomon replied that he wanted wisdom to judge the people. God replied, "Not only will I give you wisdom to make you the wisest of all men throughout time, but I will also give you riches, glory and a long life."

man spoke, "I blush that you should think me a thief. My brother lives alone and must pay workers to help him in the fields. He has hardly anything left to live on, while I have my wife and children to help me. We decided that we would give my brother a few sheaves of corn secretly, just to help him out. Now I understand why my stock of sheaves never went down. . . ."

The king, deeply touched, took the brothers in his arms, "Forgive me for thinking that you were thieves, instead of admiring your generosity. I beg of you, sell me your field, that I may build God's temple here."

The two men were happy to agree. The foundations of the temple were set where the corn and the olive tree had stood, and no further catastrophe befell the building of God's house.

Before the temple was built, ceremonies took place in a sanctuary, a holy place that guarded the Ark of the Covenant, where the scrolls of the Law were kept.

The temple was built on the summit of Mount Moriah, in what is today the Old City of Jerusalem. It took seven years to build and was a magnificent building, dedicated to God and containing the Ark. It had altars burning incense and a golden menorah. It was a place of pilgrimage three times a year for the entire people of Israel.

A couple trusted in the advice of a wise man.

Rabbi Shimon bar Yohai was a wise man who lived during Roman times. In order to escape persecution, he and his son spent twelve years in a cave, studying the Torah. Afterwards, everyone came to them for advice, as they were famous for their wisdom, goodness, and justice.

One day a married couple came to see them. "Rabbi," said the husband, "my wife and I have lived together for ten years in loving harmony, but we have not managed to have a child. Because of this, we have decided to separate."

"When you got married," said the Rabbi, "you held a great feast. Do the same for your separation, then come

back to me and I will pronounce your divorce."

Then the Rabbi took the husband aside and whispered to him: "After the feast, ask your wife to take away with her the most precious thing in your home."

The feast was a great success, and when it was over, the husband thanked his wife for the years of happiness they had spent together and asked her to choose the most precious thing in the house to take to her father's house. That done, the man laid down with a heavy heart and fell asleep.

As soon as he was asleep, the wife called the servants and had her sleeping husband carried on his bed to her father's house. When the man woke up, he was startled to find himself in a different place from that in which he had gone to sleep the night before. His wife smiled and explained, "Did you not ask me to take away with me the most precious thing in the house? Well, you are the most precious thing in the world to me."

At that time, it was usual for a divorced woman to go back to her father's house. A woman on her own would have had no protection.

Here the problem of sterility is treated by speech, freeing whatever has stopped the body from functioning properly. Husband and wife needed to say in words just how much they meant to each other.

The couple went back to Rabbi Shimon. "Thank you, Rabbi, for your wise advice. Please bless us now, that we may have a child."

That same year, they had a son, whom they called Shimon.

Maimonides, a highly regarded doctor from Cordoba, is asked . . .

According to Jewish tradition, men are called by their name, followed by their father's name. Moses ben Maimon means Moses son of Maimon.

Entrance to the mosque in Cordoba.

Dalet is the fourth letter in the Hebrew alphabet and the number 4. Its name means doorway, but its original drawing represented a fish, then a fish head, a shape which is kept to this day in the Greek delta.

This story comes from an oral tradition going back 900 years.

Maimonides is the Latin form of Moses ben Maimon, also known as Rambam. Famous philosopher, doctor, and wise man, he wrote many works, among them the *Guide for the Perplexed.* He also summarized the Jewish faith into thirteen articles.

A long time ago, in the twelfth century, there lived in Cordoba a very wise man called Moses ben Maimon. He was a leader of the Jews, protecting them in their exile. He was also an excellent doctor and had healed kings.

Having heard of Maimonides's great talents, the sultan of Egypt wanted him to replace his personal physician, who had just died. Maimonides agreed to take the post, not realizing that he was walking into a viper's nest: the best doctors in Egypt had been waiting to be chosen as the sultan's physician, and they all joined together in their

Portrait of
Maimonides,
from an Israeli
stamp.

Jews lived in
Cordoba
following the
Muslim conquest
of Spain in 711.

loathing of Maimonides and set about trying to ruin him.

One day, they said to Maimonides, "We are such great doctors, that we can restore the sight of someone who has been blind from birth!"

Maimonides replied, "Impossible! Only those who have been made blind through illness or an accident can have their sight restored."

The others challenged him in front of the sultan, "We are going to prove that we are greater doctors than Maimonides, and that he is nothing but a braggart." They brought a blind man before the sultan, and sprinkled his eyes with a preparation they had made. The man leaped up joyfully, proclaiming, "I can see for the first time, I am healed!"

Sultan was the name for a king in some Muslim countries.

The doctors stood triumphantly before the sultan, who gazed suspiciously at Maimonides. Maimonides took a scarf out of his pocket and waved it before the man, asking, "What is this?"

"A red scarf," replied the man.

Maimonides smiled victoriously. "How can you know what color it is if you have been blind from birth, as you claim?"

The sultan realized that he had been tricked and sent Maimonides's enemies away. But they did not give up their campaign of lies against him. In the end, the sultan's advisors suggested that he should have another doctor, Kamun, to keep an eye on Maimonides.

Maimonides was born in Cordoba in 1135 and died in Cairo in 1204.

The sultan did not want two doctors and

decided to put them to a devilish test, "I want to find out which of you is the better doctor. Your test is as follows: whichever of you succeeds in poisoning the other will have proved that he is the better

But there are enemies watching him.

doctor, and he will stay with me as my personal physician."

Kamun went off happily: he had already poisoned several people and had no scruples about getting rid of the Jew who stood in his way. But Maimonides neither wanted to die, nor to kill. He spent many days and nights trying to think up a solution, but without success.

Kamun quickly mixed a powerful poison and slipped it into his enemy's food. But Maimonides immediately mixed the appropriate antidote and appeared to be none the worse. He just kept on working steadily, trying to avoid the various potions served to him by his enemy. Nonetheless, every time Maimonides met Kamun he would say to him, "Watch out, I've got something for you."

Kamun waited in dread to find out what his indestructible enemy had prepared. In the meantime, he mixed every known antidote, swallowing them one after another. But still he could not detect poison anywhere. He thought perhaps he had been given some slow-acting poison which he had swallowed unsuspectingly. He decided to drink nothing but milk drawn from the goat before his very eyes. He

The interdiction against murder is the sixth of the Ten Commandments, or *Decalogue*. This text makes up the Law given by God to Moses, and forms the foundation of Judaism, and later of Christianity and Islam.

Medicinal plant from Asia Minor.

started to tremble with weakness. He no longer had the strength to prepare poisons. Then, one day, Kamun was holding the pot of freshly drawn milk when Maimonides came up, looking as healthy as ever. Maimonides gazed at the pot and said, "Ah, so that's what you're drinking!"

Kamun boiled with anger, sure that he was lost, "I've swallowed his poison! He's managed to get it into the milk! Quick, I must mix an antidote!"

But weakened as he was, the fury of his rage killed him where he stood, and he fell dead at Maimonides's feet.

Everyone wanted to know what the extraordinary poison had been, but Maimonides gave the rest of the milk in Kamun's pot to a small child, who kept on playing happily. Then they accused Maimonides of witchcraft and demanded he be put to death.

Maimonides explained everything that had happened and finished by saying: "It was hatred, greed, and fear that killed Kamun."

Everyone recognized the truth of what he said. The sultan gave him his complete confidence, and nobody tried to hurt him again.

An Arab surgical saw, reprinted from a 16th-century manuscript.

Jewish morality has always held that one can only be raised by one's own success, not by the defeat of others.

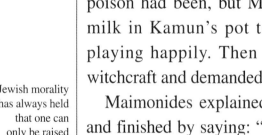

At midnight, the rabbi began his strange incantations.

The letter *he,* the fifth letter of the alphabet, is also the number 5. The original drawing of the letter showed a praying man, his arms lifted toward heaven, a shape that can still be seen in the Greek *epsilon* and in the Latin *E.* This letter occurs twice in the sacred tetragrammaton.

This story comes from an oral tradition dating back to the 16th century.

The creation of the Golem is attributed to Rabbi Loew (1525–1609), known as the Maharal. He wrote works of philosophy and mysticism.

According to the position of the moon, it was nearly midnight, the hour we had been waiting for.

But my master, the Maharal of Prague, wanted to hear the baying of the dogs, because, according to the teachings of the Talmud passed on to us by Rabbi Eliezer, "The night can be divided into three: at the end of the first part, the ass will bray; at the end of the second part, the dogs will bay; at the end of the third part, the nursing child will suckle, and man and wife together chuckle."

At the place where we were standing, the river flowed

The Talmud is a collection of Jewish law, discussions, and traditions. The collection includes sayings of the great master Rabbi Eliezer.

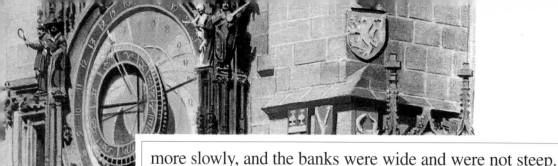

more slowly, and the banks were wide and were not steep. I saw by the light of the moon, which was perfectly round on this fifteenth night of the first month of spring, my master, seated, his eyes firmly shut, facing the east. He had passed the first part of the evening in meditation, prayer, and immersion. He had asked me to prepare myself. The night was bitterly cold.

As the dogs' first baying cries rang out, he stood up quietly and solemnly. The moonlight threw his long shadow starkly across the ground. Here and there, the snow still lay in deep drifts. He started to draw on the ground with his stick. Bit by bit, a huge figure appeared. He had started with the head, then the neck, then the arms. Halfway between head and feet, level with the navel, he stopped. He held out two great buckets toward me and said, "Go down to the river. Take this goblet, and fill the bucket you are holding in your right hand with 248 measures. Pour 365 measures into the bucket you are holding in your left hand."

I returned with my 613 measures just as my master finished drawing carefully around the feet. He took the bucket from my right hand and poured the contents over the limbs of the

It is a Jewish custom to turn to the east, toward Jerusalem and the Temple, at the moment of prayer.

The Torah is made up of 613 commandments, divided into 365 negative commandments, equal to the number of days in the year, and 248 positive commandments, equal to the number of organs in the human body.

The hours on the face of the clock on the town hall in Prague (see left), opposite the old synagogue, were written with Hebrew characters, and the hands always went backwards.

Immersion, or *mikvah,* is a ritual purification bath carried out in natural (river, rainwater, seawater) water.

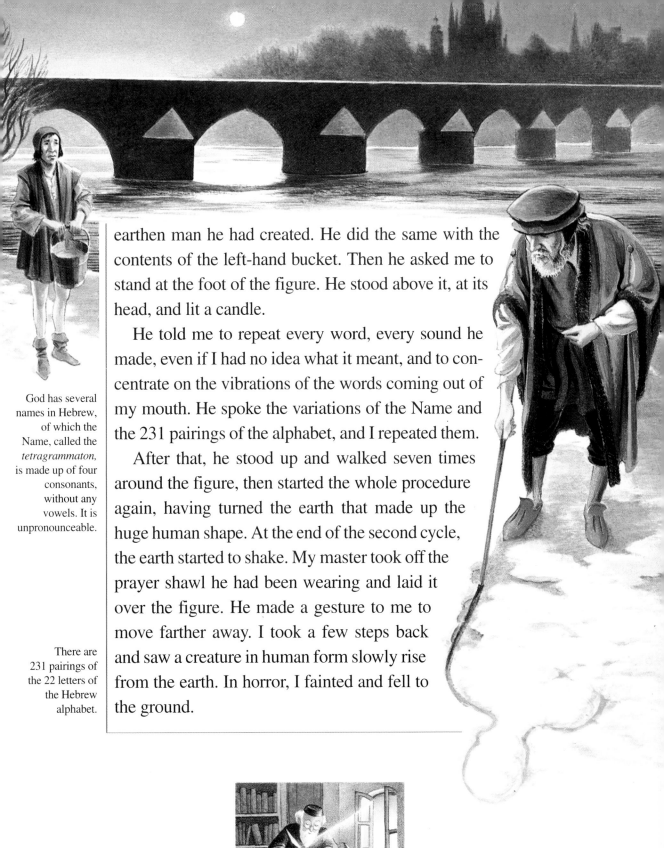

earthen man he had created. He did the same with the contents of the left-hand bucket. Then he asked me to stand at the foot of the figure. He stood above it, at its head, and lit a candle.

He told me to repeat every word, every sound he made, even if I had no idea what it meant, and to concentrate on the vibrations of the words coming out of my mouth. He spoke the variations of the Name and the 231 pairings of the alphabet, and I repeated them.

After that, he stood up and walked seven times around the figure, then started the whole procedure again, having turned the earth that made up the huge human shape. At the end of the second cycle, the earth started to shake. My master took off the prayer shawl he had been wearing and laid it over the figure. He made a gesture to me to move farther away. I took a few steps back and saw a creature in human form slowly rise from the earth. In horror, I fainted and fell to the ground.

God has several names in Hebrew, of which the Name, called the *tetragrammaton,* is made up of four consonants, without any vowels. It is unpronounceable.

There are 231 pairings of the 22 letters of the Hebrew alphabet.

Meanwhile, the Christians' hatred grew more and more wild.

Ghetto refers to the part of a town that was set aside for Jews. It was closed at night. From the 16th century to the mid-20th century, Jews were often forced to live in such separate areas. The first ghetto was set up in Venice in 1516.

The rumor spread like a forest fire. The charges were vague but obsessive: poisoning the wells, kidnapping and killing Christian children, or quite simply killing God.

In the ghetto, terrified men and women scurried to and fro. I saw my master, who ordered me to follow him, "Come quickly, the Christians are massing at the gates of the ghetto, they are going to attack."

One of the Jewish blacksmiths was organizing the defense, "Bring out your tables, all your furniture, and build a barricade at each end of every road. Let every able-bodied man arm himself as best he can. Shut the women and children inside, keep quiet and wait."

"They're coming, they're coming," came the cry, a cry which multiplied and spread through the narrow streets of the ghetto. Old people who had known the massacres of 1557 rocked and recited prayers. Soon voices were heard from the neighboring street, "Kill the yids! Kill Jesus's executioners!"

The peasants had yelled this same litany of hatred several times over the centuries. Suddenly my master, armed only with his stick, oblivious of the danger, leaped to the top of the barricades and began to speak to the maddened peasants.

Jews were falsely accused of deicide, that is, of killing Jesus. This accusation was only finally set aside by the Second Vatican Council of the Roman Catholic Church (1962–1965).

In 1541, and then in 1557, the Jews of Prague suffered expulsions and massacres. They were let into the city again in 1562.

"What do you want?" he demanded.

When they saw this tall, wise-looking man with his noble manner, the violent mob stopped dead. But one of the leaders, afraid that the moment might slip from him, shouted out rudely, "Is this old madman their rabbi? Get back, old man, if you value your life! We're going to make a few Jews dance today! Yes, and tickle a few Jewish girls!"

My master wanted to say something more, but the mob took up the cry, "Killers, Christ killers, poisoners of wells!"

My master spoke out above their cries in a powerful voice, "You will kill no one here today, nor tomorrow. As long as I live, you will not harm any Jew in Prague!"

The peasants froze at the sound of his voice. Nobody had dreamt of such resistance. "Go home!" said my master. "Take your pitchforks and go back to your farms!"

Even the leaders were shaken by his firmness and his resolution. They told the mob to disperse for now, saying they would be back later. No one had seen anything like it. The Jews had won several hours of respite.

Night fell. Some men stayed at the barricades to keep

Jews were accused of profaning the host and of poisoning the wells with deadly sickness, like the bubonic plague. Below you can see a bonfire with Jews being burned alive (from the Nuremberg chronicles, 15th century).

The Jews, hiding in the synagogue, were about to be massacred.

guard, while most of the people took shelter in the big synagogue. The first part of the night passed in an uneasy calm, but then, just before dawn, heavy blows rang out on the synagogue doors, waking the people.

"Open up!" bayed the voices of the mob.

"Who is it? What do you want?" replied my master.

"Open up, or we'll set fire to the whole filthy building!"

The crowd huddled in the synagogue now listened in horror to the sound of straw being piled against the walls. They would carry out their threat, of that there was no doubt. Thousands of Jews had already been burned to death in the same way, in the dangerous days before Easter, in Russia, in Poland, in England, in Germany, in France, burned alive in bonfires built of hatred. My master, looking down lovingly at these poor terrified people, asked everyone to get out of the central aisle.

"Don't be afraid," he said. "You must trust in me." Blows hammered on the door. My master moved forward and lifted the heavy plank that barred the doorway. The doors swung back violently, pushed open by the press of peasants who now tumbled pell-mell into the

Jews first settled in Prague at the end of the 10th century. The Jewish quarter was created in 1142. The old synagogue (Altschul) dates from this period. It was enlarged and called *Altneuschul,* or old-new.

The Altneuschul synagogue in Prague.

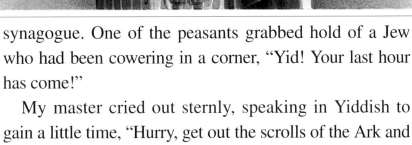

synagogue. One of the peasants grabbed hold of a Jew who had been cowering in a corner, "Yid! Your last hour has come!"

My master cried out sternly, speaking in Yiddish to gain a little time, "Hurry, get out the scrolls of the Ark and keep them safe."

The Torah is written on parchment, rolled onto two poles.

"Filthy old Jew," said the man, appearing to understand him, "stop playing about! Just wait and see what we'll do with your moldy scrolls!"

And the mob hurled itself toward the velvet curtain covering the Ark, trying to lay hands on the sacred scrolls.

Just then a huge shadow fell across everyone there, blocking out the light that had spilled into the synagogue through the open doors and covering the crowd with a terrifying darkness. Summoned in some mysterious way by its master, the Golem had appeared. In the deathly silence which had fallen, it reached down suddenly and plucked up, in each huge, powerful hand, three of the peasants. The men were too stunned to speak or move and hung there as the giant squeezed and squeezed. The sound of their bones cracking filled the synagogue.

Then it was the mob's turn to cry out in terror, as the desperate peasants struggled to escape, scrambling toward

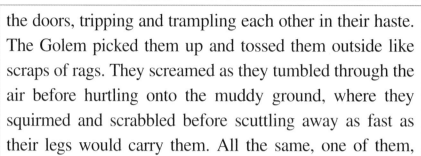

the doors, tripping and trampling each other in their haste. The Golem picked them up and tossed them outside like scraps of rags. They screamed as they tumbled through the air before hurtling onto the muddy ground, where they squirmed and scrabbled before scuttling away as fast as their legs would carry them. All the same, one of them, more dogged than the others, managed somehow to set light to the straw piled against the walls. Rabbi Loew smelled the smoke and gave a brief order to the Golem. It dropped the peasant it was holding, hurried to the fire, and stamped it out with supernatural speed. The last of the attackers took advantage of the moment to escape from the synagogue. Only the Jews remained. They could hardly believe in the miracle they had just witnessed: the Golem had saved their lives and stopped a pogrom!

Obeying a last order from its master, the Golem strode out toward the rabbi's home. They say that the rabbi returned him to dust in the cellar of his house that very night. Whatever happened, it is certain that nobody dared attack the Jews of Prague for many years to come, and it is equally certain that no Christian passed the great doors of the synagogue without crossing himself devoutly.

Defender of the poor, the weak, the humiliated, the Golem embodies hope.

Pogrom is a Russian word for a violent uprising aimed at the destruction of Jews.

The myth of the Golem is deeply rooted in Jewish tradition. It runs against the belief that Jews just let themselves be massacred without defending themselves.

Reb Shmuel received a strange legacy from his master: stories.

The letter *vav,* the sixth letter of the alphabet, is also the number 6. It is the symbol of the nail.

This 18th-century Hasidic story has been translated from Yiddish, the language of the Jews of eastern Europe.

The Baal Shem Tov was the founder of the Hasidic movement, which emphasized communal prayer, singing, and dancing.

Feeling himself on the brink of death, the Baal Shem Tov, the Master of the Good Name, decided to leave the few riches that he had to his disciples. To one he gave his prayer shawl; to another his silver snuffbox.

His most faithful servant, Reb Shmuel, waited for his turn, but the Master had given all his goods away—nothing was left.

Then the Baal Shem Tov turned toward him with a smile, "To you, I give my stories. You will travel the world over so that people may hear them."

Hat worn by Russian and Polish Jews in the 18th and 19th centuries. Opposite: prayer shawl, or *talith.*

Surprised, Reb Shmuel thanked the Master, in whom he trusted completely, without fully understanding just what it was he had been left.

The Master died.

Reb Shmuel found himself alone. He said to himself, "What kind of inheritance have I received? Stories that nobody wants to hear?"

The Sabbath is the rest day given by God. There are three special meals held on the Sabbath—supper on Friday and two meals on Saturday.

He remained alone, poorer than ever. One day a rumor began that there was a man, far away, who was prepared to pay large sums of money to hear stories about the Baal Shem Tov. Reb Shmuel found out more about it and let it be known he was the man for the job. He was sent an invitation and, after a long journey, he arrived in a big city in Russia one Friday morning. He was welcomed by his host—no less than the president of the community.

The Baal Shem Tov (Besht for short) lived in Russia in the 18th century. He died in Medzibozh, in Podolia, in 1760.

That same evening, the president gathered all his friends together to join in a grand Sabbath meal prepared in honor of their special guest. As the meal was drawing to a close, the president stood up and said: "We have the honor to have in our midst the secretary and disciple of the Baal Shem Tov, who has come amongst us especially to tell us stories of his Master. Reb Shmuel, please tell us more."

Reb Shmuel stood up, deeply moved to be able to

One day, he heard that someone longed to hear them.

speak about his beloved Master at last. He looked over his audience warmly and wanted to start telling them some of his stories. He opened his mouth to speak and, horrors! Nothing! His mind had gone blank! He could not remember a single story, not even the tiniest memory.

The president, seeing him upset, said, "Reb Shmuel must be worn out after his long journey. After a good night's sleep he will be himself again, and he will be able to remember some excellent stories to tell us."

The next day, in the middle of the second meal of the Sabbath, Reb Shmuel stood up to speak, and, once again, nothing. Embarrassed and upset, he sat down again. The president, once more, was kind and understanding, and promised the assembly that all would go well during the third meal.

But during the third meal the same thing happened, and the next morning Reb Shmuel, bitterly ashamed, found himself setting out on his journey home. His host was cold and distant toward him, and few people came out to wish "good journey" to the man whom the whole town had named "the man with no stories."

The horses had already set off at a brisk pace when Reb Shmuel stood up on the sledge and shouted, "Stop,

stop! I've got a story!"

The horses were reined in and, standing up where he was, Reb Shmuel said to the president, who was looking at him with a spark of hope and interest, "It's just a small anecdote, I'm not sure if it would interest you."

The president encouraged him with a slight nod of his head.

"It was a winter's night. The Baal Shem Tov woke me, 'Reb Shmuel, harness the horses, we're going out.'

"We traveled through the icy snow, across deep forests until, after several hours, we arrived at a large, very beautiful house. The Master went in and, after only half an hour, he came out. 'We're going home!' he said."

As the story ended, the president started sobbing convulsively. Reb Shmuel looked at him in amazement.

Through his tears, the president could see the astonished faces of the men around him, "Let me explain. The person that the Baal

Hasidism is a popular religious movement that emerged in Judaism in the second half of the 18th century. Followers lived in close-knit groups headed by charismatic leaders.

Shem Tov was visiting that night was me! At that time, I had a very important position in the Christian church. My job was to organize forced conversions, events which always occurred with violence.

"When the Baal Shem Tov burst into my home on that memorable night, I was preparing one of the cruelest decrees of my whole career. He had hardly crossed the threshold when he began saying in a voice that grew louder and louder and more and more passionate, 'How long will this go on? How long will you torture your own brothers? Didn't you know that you yourself were a Jewish child, rescued from a pogrom, taken in by a Polish family who kept your origins a secret? The time has come to return to your brothers and your tradition!'

"I was overwhelmed and immediately decided to leave everything and start my life again from scratch. I asked the Master, 'But will there come a day when I shall be forgiven for my crimes?'

"The Baal Shem Tov replied, 'The day that somebody tells you this story, that is the day when you will know you have been forgiven.' "

This story explains that people cannot have a future without forgiveness. They stay locked in the past, as in a prison. Forgiveness plays a central part in Jewish religion and in Jewish thinking.

Forced conversion to Christianity was one of the persecutions to which Jews were subjected. It also happened that Jewish children were kidnapped, baptized, and brought up in convents or in Christian families, who were convinced that they were doing the right thing.

WHAT IS JUDAISM?

The oldest texts to have come down to us were found tucked into jars that had been hidden in a cave at Qumran, near the Dead Sea.

The Bible, written 2,500–3,500 years ago, contains the history of the Jewish people, who in earlier times were known as the Hebrews. It also sets out laws, social rules, and religious rites.

Judaism is based on texts, laws, stories, and rituals. These bind together a society that believes in a single God and is founded on principles of justice and mutual respect. The Jewish God is not an abstract power, but a force closely involved in the world and in the history of humanity.

Written Law, or *Tanakh*

The Hebrew bible (Jews call it *Tanakh*) forms the basis of the Jewish faith. It consists of twenty-four books grouped in three sections: the Torah, the Prophets, and the Writings. Judaism is marked by its great devotion to the Bible, or written Law, and by its willingness to develop new commentaries on it.

The Torah

The first five books of the Bible, which are called the *Torah* in Hebrew, are seen as the most important part of Jewish scriptures. The Torah contains all the laws that have united the Jews throughout the centuries.

Oral Law (Talmud or Midrash)

The Jews needed help in understanding how to apply the Law to their lives, so the rabbis interpreted the laws for them. In the 2nd century they were developed into texts called the Mishnah, or Teaching.

Two great intellectual centers of the time—Babylon and Jerusalem—gave rise to different interpretations of the Mishnah. These commentaries became the Babylonian Talmud and the Jerusalem Talmud. Completed in the 6th century, the Talmud is the text referred to for religious practices, the organization of society, and the development of philosophy.

At the same time, another text developed, the Midrash. It helps explain Bible stories by defining words, adding parables, and emphasizing the origins of rituals.

The Torah, or Law, given to Moses on Mount Sinai 3,400 years ago, contains the Ten Commandments: You shall have no other gods before me; You shall not make for yourself a graven image; You shall not take the name of the Lord your God in vain; Remember the Sabbath day; Honor your father and your mother; You shall not kill; You shall not commit adultery; You shall not steal; You shall not bear false witness; You shall not covet.

Top center:
The creation of
the world, taken
from the Sarajevo
Haggadah,
16th century.

4,000 YEARS OF TRADITION

AND HISTORY

The probable
route taken by
the Hebrews
from Egypt to the
Promised Land.

Year 1, in the
Jewish calendar,
corresponds to
the creation of
the world, which
is placed at
3,988 B.C.

The revelation of the one God

According to Jewish tradition, before the world as we know it came to exist, there was nothing but darkness and chaos. God created the world in six days: Adam and Eve were created on the sixth day, and on the seventh day, he created rest. They were expelled from the Garden of Eden for eating the forbidden fruit of the tree of knowledge of good and evil.

Then came Cain, Adam and Eve's firstborn son, who murdered his brother Abel. Their third son, Seth, was an ancestor of Noah. Noah escaped in his ark when a flood destroyed the rest of humanity.

Ten generations later, in Chaldea, we find Abraham, believer in the one God. He settled in Canaan. Of his sons, Ishmael became the ancestor of all the Muslim Arabs, while Isaac became head of a long line: his son Jacob had twelve sons and one daughter. One of these sons, Joseph, sold as a slave by his brothers, was taken to Egypt where his wisdom and ability to interpret dreams raised him to the rank of viceroy. When a famine ravaged Canaan, Jacob and his other sons joined Joseph in Egypt. Their descendants were enslaved by the Egyptians for more than two hundred years.

The birth of the Hebrew people

It was Moses who received a divine mission from God to free his people from slavery. Leaving Egypt was the

When God told
Abraham that he
would have many
descendants, he
also told him that
they would spend
400 years
enslaved in Egypt.
They had to be
exiled before they
became a people.
They experienced
what it was like
to be a stranger
in a strange land,
so that they might
always respect
strangers.

In the Middle
Ages, Jews were
forced to wear
different clothes
to set them apart
(like the hat worn
by King David in
the illustration
below). Later,
they were forced
to wear a yellow
star.

2332: The flood (according to Jewish tradition).
2000: Birth of Abraham.

1320: Exodus from Egypt. Moses is given the Law on Mount Sinai.

1280: Arrival in the Promised Land. Conquest of Jericho.
1030: Saul, first king of the Hebrew people.

1010 to 970: Reign of King David.
1000: Jerusalem, political and spiritual capital.

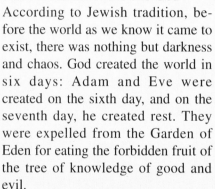

The Temple of Jerusalem had just been restored and extended by Herod the Great when it was destroyed in 70 A.D.

founding event of the Jewish people. Once out of Egypt, Moses led the people into the Sinai desert, where the Torah, or Law, was revealed to them. For more than forty years, the Hebrews wandered in the desert, within sight of the Promised Land. Joshua then conquered Israel, where the Hebrews settled.

The twelve tribes of Israel were led by the Judges—often military leaders chosen to fight off invaders.

A royal house

Samuel was both judge and prophet. He set up a central government and chose two warriors, Saul and David, as kings. They finally cleared the land of enemies. Solomon, David's son and his successor, built the temple in Jerusalem.

The schism

After Solomon, the kingdom split in two: the kingdom of Judah and the kingdom of Israel. The prophets—Isaiah, Jeremiah, Ezekiel—called on the people to live a purer life, closer to the laws of God, or face

destruction. The kingdoms fell: Israel was conquered by the Assyrians, who deported all its inhabitants. The kingdom of Judah was conquered by Nebuchadnezzar, who carried its people off to Babylon.

Fifty years later, they returned to their own land and rebuilt the temple. For more than 400 years, the Jews once again practiced their religion. Seventy-one wise men, the Great *Sanhedrin,* governed the country and administered justice.

Conquered by the Romans

Toward the 1st century, people split into different political and religious parties: Sadducees, who only followed the written Law; Pharisees, who emphasized the sacred texts and morality; Zealots, who sought independence; and Essenes, who devoted themselves to the purification of their souls.

In 70 A.D., the Romans destroyed the second temple, which had been restored and enlarged by Herod, and the Holy City along with it.

The prophet Jeremiah, according to a Christian mosaic in Rome.

Jesus, whom Christians recognize as the Messiah, lived between 6 and 30 A.D. Christianity grew out of Judaism, but rejected many of its ritualistic constraints.

ISRAEL

JUDAH

When Solomon died, the kingdom was divided into two halves, Judah and Israel.

972 to 922: Reign of Solomon.
922: Schism between northern kingdom (Israel) and southern kingdom (Judah).

586: Destruction of the temple. Exile in Babylon.
538: Return from exile.
516: Building of the 2nd temple.

332: Alexander the Great conquers Palestine.
250: Bible translated into Greek.
139: Jewish religion forbidden.

6: Birth of Jesus.
70: Destruction of second temple by Titus. Jews are expelled.

During the 17th and 18th centuries, a number of wooden synagogues were built in Poland. Most were burned down, either deliberately or accidentally.

Rashi, the greatest commentator on the Talmud and the Torah, was born in Troyes in 1040.

The diaspora

The Jews were again exiled, expelled from Palestine by the Romans after the second temple was destroyed. They scattered through Europe, North Africa, and Asia Minor. This was a dark period for them; times of relative calm were broken with expulsions and vicious persecutions.

The Crusades

Toward the year 1000, the Turks invaded Jerusalem and the area around it, destroying Christian churches and monasteries. This drove the Christians of Europe to set out to deliver the Holy Places from the hands of the infidels. The first expedition pillaged and massacred the Jewish populations it met on its way, in England, France, and Germany. The second expedition, did the same in Israel itself.

Judaism and Islam

At first Mohammad was favorable to Judaism, and introduced into Islam laws drawn from the Torah, such as monotheism, circumcision, the non-representation of God, as well as the dietary laws. But when the Jews refused to be converted to the new religion, Mohammad changed from friendship to open hostility and massacres took place.

In the countries conquered by the Arabs, from Persia to Spain, Mohammad's successors were, by and large, tolerant of the Jews, as they were of the Christians, each being *dhimmis* (protected) in exchange for their political and military submission. So there was a golden age for the Jews up until the twelfth and thirteenth centuries. Then the next age of persecutions began.

The Inquisition

Set up in the thirteenth century by Pope Innocent III, the Inquisition had as its aim the elimination of all Christian heretics and Jews. Jews had a choice between leaving, converting, or dying. Those who chose to stay

Left, German Jews being driven out of a city in 1470.

Between the 10th and the 16th centuries, persecution and expulsions forced the Jews to flee from country to country. It was not until the 16th to 18th century that written body of popular stories developed. Hasidism was the driving force behind this; it saw the rebirth of the Midrash, which still permeates Jewish literature today.

1st and 2nd c: Mishnah composed.
3rd–6th c.: Talmud composed.
391: Bible translated into Latin.
622: Beginning of Islam.
613–694: Anti-Jewish laws in Spain.

638: Caliph Omar conquers Jerusalem.
1099: Jerusalem seized by Crusaders. Jews massacred.

1242: Saint Louis has the Talmud publicly burned in Paris.
13th–16th c.: Inquisition persecutes Jews and heretics.
1290–1597: Expulsion of the Jews from England, Spain,

France, and Italy. Numerous massacres.
1516: First ghetto set up in Venice.
1789: French Revolution. Emancipation of the Jews.

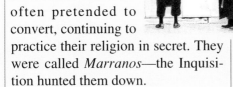

In the 18th century, a movement called Hasidism developed in Russia and Poland. It orders its followers to serve God with joy and enthusiasm. It is represented today by the Bratslav, Lubavitch, and other movements.

often pretended to convert, continuing to practice their religion in secret. They were called *Marranos*—the Inquisition hunted them down.

The pogroms

From the middle of the eighteenth century up until World War II, pogroms, or organized attacks, were widespread. In Russia, Poland, Germany, France, and England, there were sudden outbursts of hatred and violence against Jewish communities: men, women, and children, old and young alike, were massacred, their houses burned down, their synagogues profaned, their sacred texts destroyed.

Pogroms were often incited by the Christian authorities, who set the masses against the Jewish people, calling them *deicides,* that is, those responsible for the death of Jesus. Other accusations were hurled at them too. In 1648, in Ukraine, Cossacks massacred thousands of Jews.

The Shoah

During World War II, from 1939 to 1945, the persecution of the Jews reached new levels of atrocity. Across Europe, a wave of terror was unleashed. Under the leadership of Adolf Hitler, the Nazi regime and their collaborators put to death in gas chambers over six million Jews of all ages and from every corner of Europe. This was the *shoah,* or holocaust. The memories of the horror and grief of this time haunt Jews to this day.

Top center: Praying at the only remaining part of the temple, the Western Wall, usually called the *Wailing Wall,* is an act of renewal for Jews.

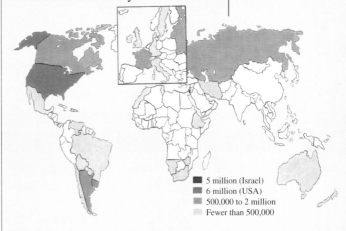

■ 5 million (Israel)
■ 6 million (USA)
■ 500,000 to 2 million
Fewer than 500,000

Distribution of Jews in the world today.

1917: Balfour Declaration promises the Jews a national homeland in Palestine.
1939–1945: World War II. Six million Jews die in Nazi concentration camps.

1946: The *Exodus,* carrying 4,515 Jews trying to reach Israel, is returned to Hamburg by the British.
1948: Independence of the state of Israel. Neighboring Arab countries declare war on it.

1967: Six Day War; reunification of Jerusalem.
1973: Yom Kippur War.
1979: Peace treaty between Egypt (President Sadat) and Israel (Prime Minister Begin).

1989: Mass emigration of Russian Jews to Israel.
September 1993: Israeli-Palestinian Peace Accord.

RITUALS AND STORIES

This seven-branched candelabra, or menorah, was painted in the 1st century in Rome.

Rules *(kosherim)* govern what Jews can eat and how food should be prepared. Milk and meat should never be mixed, and eating some animals is forbidden.

Above, the purification of utensils that have been used for serving nonkosher food, in a communal cauldron. (14th century)

How rituals began

A story is a memory. It becomes a tradition when it gets passed down through the generations, accompanied by actions, or rituals.

The Bible story of Jacob is reinforced by a dietary ritual. In this story, Jacob, fleeing from his brother Esau, whom he had cheated out of his inheritance, crossed the river Jabbok. There he fought with an angel. He won, but during the fight he was touched on the hip, and he limped from then on. The angel blessed him and said, "Thy name shall be called no more Jacob, but Israel (which means strong against God): for as a prince hast thou power with God and with men, and hast prevailed." The Bible goes on, "Therefore the children of Israel eat not of the sinew that shrank, which is upon the hollow of the thigh, unto this day: because he touched the hollow of Jacob's thigh in the sinew that shrank."

The ritual of circumcision reminds Jews of the bond between God and Abraham.

Festivals

• The Sabbath (Shabbat): From Friday at sundown to sundown on Saturday, the Sabbath commemorates the seventh day of creation, when God rested. It is a day dedicated to study and prayer. All work is forbidden.

• Passover (Pesach) commemorates the freeing of the Hebrews from their slavery in Egypt. For a week, all leavened food, baked with yeast, is forbidden. Jews eat matzah, un-leavened bread.

Some religious feasts begin by blowing the shofar.

Bar mitzvah: at age thirteen, a Jewish boy is committed to the religion. He receives the tefilin (small boxes holding lines of the Torah) and the *talith,* or prayer shawl. The ceremony for girls is called a Bat mitzvah.

The mezuzah, containing a roll of parchment wit[h] text from the Torah, is affixed to the doorways [of] Jewish homes.

Chanukah, the feast of lights, is held in December. It lasts for eight days. Each day a new candle is lit.

• Pentecost (Shavuoth) commemorates the revelation of the Torah on Mount Sinai. It takes place fifty days after Passover.

• The New Year (Rosh Hashanah) is celebrated in September. The shofar (a ram's horn trumpet recalling Abraham's sacrifice) is sounded to call people to meditation, for it is a ten-day period of penitence ending with Yom Kippur. On this day, dedicated to fasting and prayer, every person asks forgiveness for their sins.

• The Feast of Shelters (Sukkot) lasts for a week and recalls how God protected the Hebrews during their wanderings in the desert, after they left Egypt. All the meals are taken inside leaf-covered shelters, recalling the fragility of any house. People hold bunches made of the branch of a palm tree, sprigs of myrtle and willow, and a citron, symbols of how the people are one, though diverse.

The heart of the festival: the story

Bible stories have been passed on faithfully down the generations, thanks to the texts. But at the same time, changes, additions, and variations have gathered around the stories, building up a whole body of folklore and legend. These stories

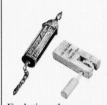

make up the Midrash. Today this means all traditional stories, whether spoken or written.

Some Jewish ceremonies revolve entirely around story telling—for instance, the evenings of Passover. In the stories that are told then, Passover answers the question foretold in the Bible: "And when your children shall say to you, 'What do you mean by this service?' you shall say, 'It is the sacrifice of the Lord's passover.'" (Exodus, 12).

The festival of Purim is celebrated with songs, dances, and disguises. The scroll relates how Esther (pictured left in an 18th-century manuscript) saved her people when they were threatened with extinction by Antiochus IV.

Each time the horrible minister Haman is mentioned as the story is read, the children make a noise with their rattles (above).

Below: Celebration of Sukkot at the Wall in Jerusalem.

Look for other titles in this series:

I WANT TO TALK TO GOD
A Tale from Islam

CHILDREN OF THE MOON
Yanomami Legends

THE RIVER GODDESS
A Tale from Hinduism

THE PRINCE WHO BECAME A BEGGAR
A Buddhist Tale

THE SECRETS OF KAIDARA
An Animist Tale from Africa

SARAH, WHO LOVED LAUGHTER
A Tale from the Bible

JESUS SAT DOWN AND SAID . . .
The Parables of Jesus